Elizabeth Mosier

THE PLAYGROUP

Elizabeth Mosier is the author of the novel, *My Life As a Girl,* as well as numerous short stories, articles, essays, and reviews, which have appeared in *Child, Seventeen, The Philadelphia Inquirer* and *Poets and Writers.* A graduate of Bryn Mawr College and the MFA Program for Writers at Warren Wilson College, she has twice been named a Discipline Winner by the Pew Fellowships in the Arts and has received a grant from the Pennsylvania Council on the Arts. Elizabeth Mosier lives outside Philadelphia with her husband and two children, and teaches creative writing at Bryn Mawr College.

First published by GemmaMedia in 2011.

GemmaMedia
230 Commercial Street
Boston, MA 02109 USA

www.gemmamedia.com

Printed in the United States of America

15 14 13 12 11 1 2 3 4 5

978-1-936846-05-4

Library of Congress Cataloging-in-Publication Data

Mosier, Elizabeth.
The playgroup / Elizabeth Mosier.
p. cm.
Summary: "A pointed look at the perils of motherhood"—Provided by publisher.
ISBN 978-1-936846-05-4 (alk. paper)
1. Motherhood—Fiction. I. Title.
PS3613.O77937P57 2011
813'.6—dc23

2011029940

Cover by Night & Day Design

Inspired by the Irish series of books designed for adult literacy, Gemma Open Door Foundation provides fresh stories, new ideas, and essential resources for young people and adults as they embrace the power of reading and the written word.

Brian Bouldrey
North American Series Editor

GEMMA
Open Door

For the women in my playgroup,
who were home when I needed them.

To Lainie —

Happy Birthday from
Theresa Kim!

Happy reading from me!

[illegible] '84

ONE

The Playgroup still called Sarah's house "Amy Marley's," though the Marleys had moved away from Phoenix two years before. Amy Marley, the mother of four children each spaced a year apart, loomed mythical in Playgroup. She sewed her kids' Halloween costumes, grew organic vegetables in her garden, ran a Spanish-language music circle for preschoolers, and started a coed scout troop. Occasionally, the other mothers attempted such feats, inspired by sadistic editors of glossy parenting magazines. But Amy did these things routinely, without instruction or applause.

Whenever Sarah and her husband David had dropped by before the closing date, they'd found Amy making cookies with her boys or building a fort with her girls or writing a letter by hand at an antique desk. Sarah couldn't dislike her; Amy was too generous and kind. But Sarah, hugely pregnant with her first child, was seized with panic whenever she encountered Amy. She wasn't ready to be a mother, and admiring Amy gave her pain.

On one such occasion, when Amy had offered her a homemade bagel, Sarah had begun crying. Warbling through the post-nasal mucous that plagued her all through her pregnancy, she confessed that she would make a terrible mother. She had no experience or even an example, as her mother had abandoned her family when Sarah was eight years old.

And she was sure that David had married the wrong person. Sarah was a woman who was grateful for factory-baked bread and takeout food. She would have preferred a new house to this old one with its leaky roof and long history etched into the adobe walls.

Amy had offered Sarah tissues and waited for her to exhaust herself. Then she'd given her a cup of tea steeped with lemon verbena picked from her garden. "A new coat of paint will make this place yours," she'd said.

But when the Playgroup first visited to welcome Sarah and her new baby to the neighborhood, we could still feel Amy's presence in every room. Sarah was defensive. That day, everything she did and said flashed "Under New Management" like a neon sign. "That cactus is going," she informed us, as I untangled the pink banner—WELCOME LIZA—that had torn free from the door and caught itself on the prickly pear in her desert-landscaped front yard. "Child Pro was here this morning," she explained, as if to convince us of her authority over her new domain. "They plugged the sockets, locked the windows, latched the cabinets, and left me with a checklist of household hazards."

Sarah led us into the living room, an arrangement of white chairs and a couch on a white pile rug. The style suited the prairie-style bungalow better, I thought, than our friend Amy's overstuffed couch and tea-rose drapes had. Another group, gathered for a different purpose, might have praised the room's stark furnishings, but we were there to compare and to judge. Sarah waited nervously for our review.

Bryn said, "It's really different."

"It's so clean," I said. "How?"

Linda said, "Good luck keeping it that way with toddlers running around. I guess Child Pro skipped the part about kid-proof furniture."

"This room's just for grownups," Sarah said. She still believed in boundaries, as only non-mothers and new mothers can.

"Better put up a gate, then," said Linda. "After Playgroup, it takes me all afternoon to clean up the mess."

"That's because you sterilize the toys," Bryn said, pursing her lips like a goat's.

Sarah laughed along with us, though she admitted later that she planned to do the same when it was her turn to host.

We seated ourselves and placed our baked goods and baby gifts on the coffee table. In the center of the table was a hammered silver bowl filled with a tangle of colored silk cord. This decoration, stolen from *House Beautiful,* gave Sarah hope. She'd been a painter before she became an art therapist, she told us. One of her bleak landscapes leaned against a still-sealed box of kitchen utensils and a bag of hideous baby clothes lent to her by her sister-in-law. She had no idea where her brushes and canvases were. And so, in that strange time, the tangled cord in the silver bowl proved that beauty was somehow still attainable.

This was important to Sarah. Most days, all her time and energy went into emptying her breasts, changing Liza's diapers, and trying to get the baby to sleep so she could take a shower.

We were still strangers then. As we talked the way strangers do—about the neighborhood and the public schools and September's lingering heat—Sarah lifted the baby from her carrier and began awkwardly preparing to feed her. She draped a receiving blanket over her shoulder for modesty, but she couldn't find her nipple without looking down. As she struggled not to call attention to what she was doing, the baby began fussing—the prelude to a lusty, magnificent scream.

"So," asked Linda over the clamor, "have you had any problems nursing?"

She'd given up on breastfeeding after three dark days she referred to as her "Confinement in the Mama Bear Cave."

"I had a little soreness," Sarah admitted, grimacing as her red-faced, sputtering baby latched onto her armpit, then onto one of her ribs. "The lactation consultant at the hospital recommended hot compresses, and that helped a bit."

"Good for you," said Linda, though her personal motto was "Formula or infanticide."

"It's the most natural thing in the world," said Bryn. She'd allied herself with the La Leche League on the issue, though she'd never actually read the League's pamphlet, which had turned to pulp in the bottom of her diaper bag.

"Natural? I was a freak," I said. "So

full I could have fed Africa. Cole nearly drowned!"

"Laurie exaggerates," Bryn said. "She's a *writer*."

"I'm not exaggerating," I said. I cupped one breast and swiveled my torso like an oscillating garden hose. "I swear! My husband had to wear a face mask when we had sex."

Sarah's expression registered alarm—*Sex?* she was thinking. *I'm supposed to have sex?*—as the baby pummeled her with tiny fists. In the commotion, the blanket slipped, Sarah's sore breast was revealed, and the baby finally found her mark. Sarah gasped with the still-surprising sting.

"They're so sweet when they're nursing," Bryn said.

I said, "Cole's eyes used to roll back in his head like a shark's during a kill."

"Look away, Bryn," said Linda. "Remember how fertile you are."

Bryn tried her best to ignore us. "Use nursing pads for the leaks," she said to Sarah. "But only the kind with hypoallergenic lanolin." I'd known Bryn a long time, since before she'd joined the corporate world, and she'd never been able to resist the killjoy urge to problem-solve.

"The allergenic ones are cheaper," I said. "And you can reuse them as biodegradable menstrual pads."

Later, Sarah told me she knew in that moment that we would be good friends. She thought I couldn't have lost myself entirely to motherhood if I'd managed to keep my sense of humor. For this reason, Sarah sought me out apart from the other women in Playgroup, confided in me and then, inevitably, began to resent me.

But this quick-burning resentment was nothing compared to the ruinous envy she secretly harbored for Amy Marley, from whom she had acquired the bones of a house but not the maternal spirit that would make it her home.

* * *

Amy Marley had started our Playgroup to teach the neighborhood preschoolers to play nicely. Actually, it was the kids' mothers who needed to learn from each other how to behave. Motherhood is like a second adolescence, a time when the self a woman thinks she owns is repossessed by so-called authorities. She's left naked and defenseless, asking herself questions about purpose, faith and identity she thought she'd already tamed. Eventually, out of sheer exhaustion, she starts asking questions that can be answered: Where do your kids go to nursery school? Do Time Outs work? Does my long hair make me seem like I'm trying to look young?

Every week at Playgroup we discussed, debated and decided these practical matters. But more philosophical questions smoldered just beneath the surface of our conversations, waiting to flame during an overwrought season such as Christmas. At times, we seemed less like mothers than like insecure teenagers at a beer keg tapping liquid courage, though at Playgroup we swilled coffee while we sought each other's advice. Amy Marley haunted all of our houses, not just Sarah's. Her spirit was conjured every time we discussed naps or discipline or toilet teaching, every time someone asked, "What would Amy Marley do?"

Amy Marley had her four children early, before she'd gotten used to nice clothes or fine dining or reading the newspaper without interruption. Amy Marley didn't drag her kids to fifteen nursery school interviews, but simply signed them up at the closest one. Amy Marley let her kids wear shorts to school in winter if they wanted, because she knew that hard experience fostered common sense. She didn't make them eat vegetables, and so they ate them eagerly.

She didn't keep a scrapbook, but instead tossed family photographs into an old suitcase, trusting memory to match each treasured image with its story. Amy Marley never mourned who she'd been before she had her children. She meant it when she said that raising her family was her calling.

Amy Marley was a perfect mother.

Mind you, the meaning of "perfect" was disputable in Playgroup. We used the word to describe the exceptional (a "perfect" day or game or score) and the commonplace (a "perfect" baby with ten fingers and ten toes) and the impossible (a "perfect" mother). If you ask me, seeking perfection through motherhood—an experience guaranteed to age and cleave and impoverish a woman—is not only pointless, it's painful. Especially for Sarah, who had vowed after her brother's death at seventeen not to have children at all.

But the propagation of our species is indebted to irony. And once she'd signed on, Sarah desperately wanted to believe in the myth of motherly perfection spread by unchecked stories of "textbook labor," "natural childbirth," "family daycare," and "work-life balance." Besides, she'd already been corrupted by her profession's prescription-pad model of contentment. She didn't dare destroy the idol our Playgroup embraced.

It would have been easier for Sarah to dismiss Amy Marley as a retro-feminist than to covet what she had. But Amy's story simply didn't fit the frame. She had not been diverted from "more serious" pursuits to raise children or dislodged from the home she'd made to indulge her husband's midlife whimsy. She'd been eager for the move from Arizona to New Mexico and grateful for the chance to begin again. Two seasons of Christmas cards had confirmed for us that she'd settled into an enviable life at the Albuquerque Academy, where her husband taught history and their children received a discounted private education.

And so we would all be surprised to find Amy Marley back at Playgroup two years later, on the day before Christmas, burdened with the weighty cargo of regret.

TWO

Twenty-eight weeks pregnant with her second child, Sarah felt that morning like she'd been abandoned in the hormonal wilderness, left to an invincible hunger, nausea and otherworldly fatigue. It seemed entirely plausible to her that her mind would leave her, too.

She'd been distracted to begin with. First, she doubted she could manage two children and her work as an art therapist at The Moorings Center for Adolescent Psychology. She'd struggled since Liza's birth to keep her work and home lives separate, to find kind and capable sitters, to feel professional and not guilty. Gradually, she'd downshifted at Moorings from five days to three days to two days per week. Still, wherever she was, she felt like she should be somewhere else. In session with Ariel (her favorite anorexic), she fretted about her daughter, Liza, who refused any food but buttered noodles. Tucking Liza into bed at night, she pictured Ariel in the vast, empty house depicted in her drawings, seated alone at a dinner table covered with sloping piles of her parents' legal briefs. Sarah felt unfaithful to both client and child.

Eventually, this feeling became intolerable. And so, with David's encouragement, she'd given notice at Moorings and begun the messy process of disengaging from her clients. But as Sarah's professional life was pared away and her life as a mother appeared in relief, she was increasingly uneasy. Ariel had regressed since she'd learned of Sarah's departure plans. Liza's vocabulary had shrunk to a single word: *No*. Sarah's old cat Krazy, who suffered from hip dysplasia, had also become incontinent. Krazy blundered through the house like a drunken bicycle messenger delivering a dreaded package of toxoplasmosis.

All of this was background noise to Sarah's bigger fear. She worried about her unborn child, for a reason she'd asked me to keep secret from the others.

* * *

Sarah had passed through her first trimester with only mild morning sickness, and had cleared the prenatal screening tests for Down syndrome and spina bifida. She'd wanted a boy and she had him, according to the sonogram taken on Halloween, when she was twenty-one weeks along. We'd all seen the picture posted to the door of her refrigerator with alphabet magnets spelling out B-O-Y. There was a story hidden behind this picture, though.

That day, Sarah and David had studied the sonogram monitor in the darkened exam room, entranced by their baby's ghostly image on the screen. Sarah had been so preoccupied that she hadn't seen the technician's mouth tighten, or sensed the transducer circling one small spot on her belly as the smear of blue conducting gel went cold. In that moment when she wasn't paying attention, her routine pregnancy became risky. The technician left the room with her medical file and the radiologist came back in. This, she realized later, was the fateful changing of the guards.

"We're picking up an abnormality here, a mass in your baby's abdomen," the doctor said. David, who'd been standing next to Sarah and holding her hand, sank into a chair. Sarah was afraid, too, but she felt it differently. As the doctor traced the white blur on the screen with the caliper, Sarah didn't feel surprise or anger or disbelief. She felt recognition, as if she'd expected the news.

"He's missing something?" Sarah asked. She squinted hard at the screen, seeking reassurance in her baby's bulb-shaped head, the five fingers she could count on each hand, the well-laid track of his perfect spine.

"Your baby has all the right parts," the doctor said. Gently, kindly, she told them first what was miraculously ordinary in their child: the bony dome of his skull, his face, his stomach, his kidneys, and the four chambers of his beating heart. Then she pointed to a small solid spot behind his stomach, shaped like a cashew. "But he has this extra piece," the doctor said. "It might be nothing—a lump of lung tissue or an organ duplication, such as a second stomach." Sarah was still trying to grasp this comically monstrous possibility when the doctor added, "Or it could be a benign tumor."

That idea seemed to hang in the air, baiting some terrifying, opposite truth. What Sarah understood was that the sonogram—their baby—was only a sketch. In the next nineteen weeks, anything might emerge from the screen's dark expanse to complete the picture.

David scooted his chair closer and squeezed her hand. That's when Sarah started to cry.

"It's going to be okay," David said, with a certainty that pricked her, warning of old pain far from its source.

"We don't know that," she snapped at him. "How can you just say that when you don't know it's true?"

"Sometimes a mass resolves itself," the doctor said, in her modulated, by-the-book tone. "We'll just have to wait and see."

Wait and see.

With those words, all the longing

Sarah felt in childhood returned to her as loss. She remembered her mother as a flip-pad of quick pictures: evidence left in ashtrays, in the grocery list scrawled on a Steno pad and forgotten, in the Chanel No. 5 sweetening the air of her bedroom, in the box of costume treasures on her dresser, in the Real Red lipstick tissue kiss floating in the toilet bowl. Her mother had been beautiful and important, sought after and admired and praised. In their house she had moved quickly, clack-clacking down the long tile hallway in kitten heels. Always, in Sarah's memory, getting ready or going or gone.

"Mama!" she accidentally cried out.

The sound of her own voice startled her and brought her back to the present.

When she realized she'd spoken, she felt small and ashamed.

"Sarah," David said, but she couldn't look at him. She kept her eyes on the ground instead, following the technician's soft-soled shoes as she walked the sonogram machine into a corner, like a prop from a magic show.

The doctor warned Sarah and David that technology was fallible, that it would be difficult to make a diagnosis in utero. It was even possible, she suggested hopefully, that the spot that appeared to be so real on the monitor was nothing more than a ghost in the machine.

Or.

David had to ask, and so the doctor had to answer. The mass could be malignant, she told them, a rare form of childhood cancer, which she pronounced as a long train of syllables Sarah had never heard before.

THREE

So, as the holiday season bore down upon her with its obligatory cheer, Sarah wasn't as joyful as she imagined a stay-at-home mother should be. The Spirit of Christmas found her cursing over a burnt batch of fudge, sending only reciprocal holiday cards with grinchy efficiency, and stomping out of Williams-Sonoma rather than wait in the mile-long line. When she discovered that Liza had shoplifted a silicone spatula from the store, she felt justified in keeping the stolen merchandise.

The night before, she'd dreamed of chasing a luminous, winged car into the desert. Her colleagues at Moorings would have called this an "easy dream," with its transparent image of missed opportunity. She'd awakened to the eerie caroling of the mourning doves, convinced she had to leave.

"Leave?" I asked in her sun-filled kitchen that morning, before the other women arrived. I'd come early to Playgroup with Hannah after dropping Cole off at nursery school, bringing a bag of hand-me-down baby clothes that I hoped would cheer her up.

"My *job*," she said.

"You quit already," I said. "Are you having second thoughts?"

"No," she said, but I could tell by the off-key tone of her voice that she was.

"Why don't you wait until after the holidays and talk to your boss again?" I said. "You'll know more then about what the mass is and what the baby needs." I knew her work was important to her. I didn't say it at the time, but I thought quitting Moorings was a big mistake that only amplified her fear.

And to hear Sarah talk, there was plenty for a mother to worry about. In that unusually dry Christmas season, wildfires raged in the mountains surrounding Phoenix. The *Arizona Republic* printed awful, irresistible tales: a PTA treasurer kidnapped her best friend's child to pay off gambling debts, a Gilbert woman drowned her newborn twins in the tub, a foster mother in Prescott nearly starved her four boys to death. In our own neighborhood, an anonymous eco-terrorist was stalking SUVs, slapping stickers on bumpers that said I'M CHANGING THE

FUTURE! ASK ME HOW! Last week, Bryn's car had been tagged as her au pair idled near All Saints' Episcopal School, waiting for soccer practice to end. Bravely, the au pair had defended her employer—"She needs a big car! She has four children!"—but failed to defend Bryn's Land Rover. And so Bryn had squandered forty-five minutes of quality time scraping stickum from her bumper and bribing the demoralized au pair with a paid vacation to Coronado.

Why did this grim news keep Sarah up at night? *She* was not a gambling, gas-guzzling psychotic! She was an artist and a member of a helping profession; she shared a fuel-efficient car with her husband, a landscape architect who biked to his downtown office on an ancient lime green Schwinn. But there were so many crimes a mother might commit unintentionally. Like the rest of us, Sarah subscribed to non-recyclable "lifestyle" magazines and used too many plastic bags. Every week, she threw away enough disposable diapers to fill her in-laws' water-wasting swimming pool. She bought organic only when other errands brought her near the Cochise Co-op with its earnest, anemic employees. Secretly, she coveted dry cleaning and aerosol hairspray. She avoided news articles about groundwater poisoning, corruption of the ozone layer, and clear evidence of climate change. And year after year, she wickedly insisted on killing a real spruce rather than buying a plastic Christmas tree or wrapping lights around a live saguaro in the southwestern tradition.

As if these deeds weren't enough to condemn her, yesterday she'd thrown away a bedspread that Liza had soiled during naptime, rather than face the gothic horror of cleaning it by hand. *What would Amy Marley do?* she'd asked herself as she tried to make sense of the mess on the bed and the clean diaper discarded on the floor. The bedspread was too large to fit into her top-loading washing machine. I told her that trashing it was morally preferable to throwing away her mischievous child.

After bathing Liza and dragging the jumbo trash bag out to the curb, Sarah had stood there for a moment wearily contemplating her life. That's when she'd spotted the old T-bird idling at the curb a half-block down the street, its engine fanning the air into a wavy mirage. It was the same model car her mother had once driven, turquoise with sinister fins and clownish round red taillights. The same car, she was convinced, that she'd seen parked outside the hospital where she had her sonograms. Encountering it for a second time in her own neighborhood, Sarah began to believe that she was being followed.

FOUR

Or that she was seeing things.

I tried to calm her down. "It's just hormones," I said. Her senses exaggerated the threat in the ordinary: a classic car, sensational headlines, job stress recast as a wish-fulfilling dream. And couldn't hormones make memories visible, too, just as they made her sense of smell as acute as a dog's? The car might be real, but insignificant, I suggested—or significant, but not real.

"I saw it," she insisted. "Twice. I know I did."

Clearly, Sarah wasn't herself. Still, though she must have felt like barring the door to the Playgroup, she warmly welcomed Linda and Maggie and Bryn when they arrived with their kids at ten o'clock. She gave the women no reason to think she was upset as they settled Chloe, Peter, and Julia on the rug scattered with Liza's sterilized toys. The women filled their mugs with fresh coffee and took their usual places at the table.

"I'm sorry about the construction noise," Sarah said. She glanced out the window to the driveway, where no vintage T-bird appeared. There was only David at work at his sawhorse and, beyond him, the neighbor boy Noah playing with his hippie-girl nanny in his front yard.

"What are you renovating this time?" asked Maggie. She flipped through the scrapbook she always brought with her, trying to find where she'd left off last time.

"Dave's building a p-l-a-y-h-o-u-s-e for Liza," said Sarah. "For Christmas. We're done fixing up *this* house." Of course she had other plans—grand, expensive schemes that would bring simplicity to their lives. Her sudden salary reduction had put these plans on hold.

"You said that three projects ago," Linda said. "You're like that Winchester rifle heiress in California. The woman who kept working on her mansion because the spirits told her to."

"This house is hardly a mansion," Sarah said.

"The Mystery House!" said Maggie. "My family went there once on vacation.

Stairs that lead to nowhere . . . windows that open onto walls . . ."

"She was trying to appease the ghosts of all the people who'd been killed with a Winchester rifle," said Linda. "Makes you wonder what terrible thing Sarah's done."

"Whatever it was, it happened a long time ago," I said, speaking up for Sarah because she looked pale. "Who has time for a life of crime between laundry loads?"

Then again, laundry itself could be criminal according to Noah's nanny, who sold low-phosphate soap as a sideline. She'd pitched her product to us at the tot lot one day, as her young charge threw sand at a baby and menaced two older children on the monkey bars. She'd also unwisely confided that Noah's mother didn't want him in our Playgroup—too many germs! And so we were compelled to extend a fresh invitation any time we encountered Evelyn.

Sarah had been refused again just yesterday. Sweaty from her struggle with the trash bag and alarmed by the appearance of the mystery car, she'd waved hello to her neighbor as she pulled up in her silver Saab. "I'm hosting Playgroup tomorrow," she'd said as Evelyn stepped out of her car balancing a Gourmet-to-Go bag and her briefcase. Her blunt-cut black hair was still perfect at the end of her workday, and her lipstick was freshly applied. "Noah's welcome, if your nanny wants to bring him."

Evelyn eyed Sarah's lunatic ensemble:

hair blasted free from its elastic band, bath-splashed T-shirt, teeth spackled with pulp from oranges she'd sucked hungrily at lunch because she didn't have the patience to peel. "I'd go nuts if I didn't work," she said. "I mean, what do those women *do* all day?"

Why didn't Sarah set her straight? Some of us worked in offices, and some of us worked at home doing what Evelyn paid her nanny to do. But as Sarah stood at the hedge dividing her desert badlands from Evelyn's golf green winter lawn, she could see that the line separating them was already definite enough.

"Are you all right?" I asked Sarah quietly, as the other mothers doctored their coffees and caught up on the neighborhood news. Bryn had discovered a new tapas place, which she described to us, plate by plate.

"I'm okay," Sarah said, though she moved and spoke like a visitor in her own body. "Just a headache, that's all."

"The best dish was silver-dollar fried breads topped with chili beans and sour cream," Bryn said.

"Indian fry bread?" said Linda. "It's been done. We ate that crap every year at the Arizona State Fair. Washed it down with RC Cola."

Sarah groaned. When I glanced at her, checking, she said, "Just hungry, I think."

"Here," I said, poking a straw through a juice box. "This will help."

But even talk of food sickened her. Just a word conjured a stomach-turning memory of a flavor: pasty pinto beans, bitter onion, rancid cooking oil, cumin-cayenne-chili sauce, cow manure, despair. Her senses made her aware of what any dog knows: that fine things are often held together by foul. Even the juice box I gave her tasted only faintly of apple and strongly of perfumed preservatives and polyethylene packaging.

Behind us, on the kitchen counter, the baby monitor crackled with static and summoned a distant voice from the air. Alarmed, Sarah stood. Still dizzy, she sat back down. "Was that someone crying?" she asked.

"It's your neighbor's cordless phone coming through your monitor," I said. "All the kids are here. Everyone's fine."

Our children played side by side on

the kitchen floor, like factory workers focused on their individual tasks. This "parallel play," as psychologists called it, might justify Noah's germ-free seclusion next door. As his mother pointed out every time she dissed us, kids didn't make real friends at this age. But Evelyn just didn't get it. Playgroup was for *us*.

"Must be hormones," Sarah said, shaking her head.

I was starting to wonder, though: was it hormones or heartbreak that made Sarah sick?

Eight weeks of uncertainty had wrecked her, and her last days at Moorings offered no relief. There, she dwelt in the sad and dangerous world her clients depicted in their therapeutic drawings: absent parents, screaming coaches, fine-print disclaimers, toxic waste, standardized testing, crippling national debt, a thirty-billion dollar diet industry, passive smoke, and professional puppet shows from which preschoolers were ejected for talking too loud. Ariel's work, in particular, was devastating—and brilliant, Sarah said. The girl had honed her skills through years of pricey art lessons. In "Petite Gourmet" cooking class, highly rated in *Professional Mother*, she'd mastered the art of French pastry and not eating. Her talent had finally landed her at Moorings, the next stop in a long line of help hired by her parents.

Sarah's own artwork, which might have steadied her, waited in another room. She'd sketched the dream car on the back of a dry cleaning receipt and clipped it to the easel in the studio she shared with the washer and dryer. She planned to paint the picture in watercolor later. Though once she'd aspired to technical perfection in her paintings, now she only hoped to understand what she'd drawn.

She hoped in vain. Though Sarah stoked her meager ambition with the idea of an afternoon Quiet Time, Liza rarely went quietly into it. Every day, Sarah conceived a new idea while she read to Liza or strolled her through our neighborhood or stirred a kid-friendly meal at the stove. Every evening, her idea perished, unpainted. She began to imagine these unborn ideas linked together like evidence of fraud—a heavy, clanging chain she'd been forging since her daughter's birth. By contrast, her work at Moorings was prolific, even profound. Ariel was her masterpiece. On good days, helping damaged children heal kept Sarah's old wounds clean and covered. On bad days, she felt her brother's suicide like a fresh tear opening into a black hole.

"You should see *my* list," Bryn was saying when I turned my attention back to the group. "The month between Thanksgiving and Christmas, I can't get anything done."

"Thanksgiving feels like ages ago," said Maggie, sighing as she sorted through die cuts of turkeys and Pilgrim hats she'd purchased to decorate her page.

"*Cranksgiving*," said Linda, scowling. "Why preserve it? It's enough to live through it once."

"Linda doesn't scrapbook," Bryn explained to Maggie.

"Is 'scrapbook' a verb now?" I asked.

"I don't look back," Linda said.

"Not even baby books for your children?" Maggie asked.

"Keeping a baby book doesn't make me a better mother," Linda said. "Don't give me that look, Bryn! Your nanny does yours."

"Au pair," Bryn said.

"I just write stuff down in whatever notebook I have in my bag," I said. "Shopping lists and notes for stories and my kids' first words, all mixed up. I know, Maggie! *Mala madre!*"

Maggie laughed. She'd just joined Playgroup in August, after ditching a church group with mandatory mother-child crafts and dismal snacks like yellowed apple slices served on flimsy paper plates. Those cheerful, well-coifed women had prayed for her during her "trial," and they expected gratitude. Maggie much preferred our "coffee group," as her daughter Julia called it, where we bickered like family and didn't flatter ourselves by thinking we could fix her after her son died of SIDS.

"Here's your chance to redeem yourself," Maggie said, handing me a sheet of red construction paper and a craft punch shaped like a leaf.

"Now I know you love me," I said.

"Only if you give it back." Maggie's

name was engraved on its handle. She'd learned that even your people—Craft Queers, she called them—would steal from you if given half a chance.

"I promise," I said.

I am not a crafter, but I understand the urge. I see myself in the women lingering in the aisles at the craft store, their eyes bright with invention, their carts piled with origami paper and glitter glue and candy molds. Seeing Maggie's supplies scattered across the table filled me with a familiar, sweet-sad feeling I usually associate with fall. "Fall feeling," I call it, for lack of a better word. Here it came at the crease of winter, warning me to hold on to the present, though I knew that to raise my children well, I had to forge ahead and begin to let go.

I went to work punching out leaves for Maggie's Thanksgiving spread. As the leaves fell to the table, Bryn raked them into a pile. Linda swiped each leaf with a glue stick and handed it to Maggie for placement. Not one of us commented on the improbability of maple leaves falling in the desert.

Into the quiet buzz of this scrapbooking bee lurched Krazy, Sarah's tabby cat. She swung wide around the turn like a city bus and whacked her loose hips on the door. Trapped in her mouth was a dark ball of David's dress socks, which she dropped at Sarah's feet like a dead mouse. "Poor Krazy," Sarah said, as she picked up the cat and cradled her. She winced at the scent of urine (real or hallucinated) clinging to the old, lame cat's leg.

Sarah's pity concealed her distress. She loved Krazy, but pregnancy's phobias made her despise the cat hair shed everywhere, the regurgitated food caulked onto the windowsill, and especially the slick litter box souvenirs she deposited around the house. Desperate, Sarah had consulted a radio pet psychologist, Dr. Phineas, who'd diagnosed the cat as depressed. "Felines are disturbed by tension," he'd said on the air, alerting her in-laws and a Moorings colleague who'd been listening in. "Is there a problem at home?"

But Sarah didn't need an expert indictment. She needed answers, absolution, and a clear protocol. And so I'd watched Liza for her one morning last week, while she sought a second opinion.

Dr. Greenwood, the humbler veterinarian, had put it simply: Krazy's hip dysplasia made it hard for her to use her litter box. "Surgery is an option," he'd advised. "But I don't recommend it. She's a sweet old girl. The best thing you can do is to make her last days more comfortable."

With that, David went to work making an open-ended litter box for Krazy, while Sarah scheduled the surgery. Their resulting argument started with the cat and netted every grievance they'd held on to in ten years of married life. Sarah only gave me the outline, but I could connect the dots. "It's expensive and ineffective," David opened, reasonably. Sarah closed with an accusation she could never take back: "You think our baby's going to die!"

No wonder she'd set aside the baby clothes I'd brought without even looking in the bag. By that point, Sarah's headache was a wild thing, like a panther pacing her frontal lobe. As she watched us labor together on Maggie's scrapbook, her face betrayed the dull pain of pointlessness and a keener desire to join in. Outside in the driveway, David stacked the lumber he'd cut for Liza's playhouse roof. He lined up the edges precisely and brushed away the loose sawdust. He worked slowly and deliberately despite his deadline, as if he were listening to the playhouse as he built it, waiting for it to reveal itself.

FIVE

Sarah hoped and David prayed for a technical error.

But with each bi-weekly sonogram, the mass became more familiar, so that eventually even Sarah could spot it easily. Her file grew thick with documentation of the abnormality, of her baby, of her. There she was, written up in the physician's report, as she and David made the rounds of meetings with specialists, asking their excellent questions about chemotherapy and home care nurses. The doctors were kind, but their scrutiny made her feel fragile. She'd assessed her clients' parents this way, as if the fault and the fix lay with them. Which is to say, with the mother.

Sarah would pass by my house on her way home from these appointments. If she saw my sitter's car in the driveway, she'd know that I was working and she wouldn't stop. Once home, she'd face a blank canvas in her studio. The soap-scented space would seem less like a studio than like a laundry room outfitted with an unopened case of watercolors and a bouquet of clean brushes arranged in a Mason jar.

On these occasions, Sarah was not filled with awe for art's healing power or faith that great works would endure. Her emotions were complicated, but summed up simply: she resented me for writing while she suffered. She felt betrayed and deserted until the next time we met at the tot lot or at Playgroup. I'd come bearing gifts—an extra iced tea or back issues of *People* or baby clothes—and we'd be friends again.

Of course, I was hardly as prolific as she imagined. Privately, I worried that having Cole and Hannah had made me sentimental and utterly ruined my work. It often struck me, as I played solitaire on my laptop while I paid a sitter to play with my kids, that writing is not living. It's a half-life spent behind a closed office door waiting for wisdom, counting on time to eventually yield fruit.

And I admit that much of the material bored me. Mommy Wars, the Mommy Track, the impossible dream of "balance": these topics were mere stand-ins for the terrible and wonderful transformation childbirth wrought.

What intrigued me was reality: Sarah's guilt over her brother's death, Linda's post-partum depression, Bryn given up for adoption, Maggie's son found blue and still in his bassinet. Was it even possible, I wondered, to capture their losses in words? Sarah still feared that there was no resolution for her life but the sad one her mother had, by her leaving, devised.

If only life worked as fiction does in revision, where the shadows of a character's life can be altered by imposing a new plot.

SIX

Nausea and the noisy argument going on in Sarah's head made the routine chaos of Playgroup unbearable, even before Bryn's daughter Chloe started to scream.

"Want cookie!" Chloe said, snatching the plastic cookie from the toy kitchen set, a gift from an unenlightened uncle.

"Mine!" said Liza, grabbing it back.

"Liza, we *share,*" Sarah said.

Liza tried offering Chloe a plastic banana, but Chloe pushed the inferior fake food away. Undaunted, Liza pressed the banana into Chloe's palm. She studied her playmate with interest, as if she understood for the first time that this girl she played with every week was not a toy, but real.

"Thank you, Liza," said Bryn. "Say thank you, Chloe."

"No!" Chloe said.

Slowly, Liza raised Chloe's hand to her mouth and bit down hard.

"Liza!" Sarah said, as Chloe began to scream.

"Chloe!" Bryn cried.

"It was an accident," Sarah said.

"Oh my God!" said Bryn. She knelt down beside Chloe to examine the wound. "Did she break the skin?"

"Bun," said Liza.

"No!" Sarah reprimanded her, though Chloe's plump white hand did resemble a fresh-baked roll, marked by a perfect impression of Liza's upstairs teeth.

"Bun!" Liza insisted, crying and hugging Sarah's knees.

"I seem!" Chloe screamed.

"It's all right," Bryn said. "She's not bleeding." Still, her irritation was evident as she carried Chloe to safety.

"They were playing so nicely," Sarah said meekly, attempting to stand with Liza still attached to her leg. "Is she okay?"

"She's fine," Bryn said. "You're fine," she told Chloe.

"I seem, I seem, I seem!" Chloe cried.

"What do you *want*?" Bryn asked, exasperated.

"Want ice cweam," Liza said.

Chloe nodded tearfully, grateful to be understood.

And so Amy Marley's unexpected appearance at the back door, just as Sarah served up ice cream sandwiches we'd agreed to call brunch, was a welcome distraction. Our children watched warily as we descended upon our old friend, hugging her and patting her back. "No hit!" Chloe scolded, her mouth full of ice cream, until we finally pulled apart.

* * *

The kitchen Amy entered surprised even Sarah, as she saw it afresh through Amy's eyes. She hadn't imagined herself to be the kind of person who would buy into the Sub-Zero fridge sales pitch or join the cult of the six-burner catering stove. The truth was she hated cooking, and so she fell for any culinary tool that promised to transform meal preparation into high art. She'd ordered the kitchen whole from a designer's showroom, right down to the homey ceramic apothecary jars. So far, though, the room had failed to inspire. The kitchen was a convincing stage set that Sarah kept very clean and rarely used.

"Wow," Amy said.

"I know, it's too much," Sarah said. During the renovation, she'd endured the Playgroup's tales of the seven-course meal Amy had made for her husband's 40th birthday, unhindered by harvest gold appliances and insufficient counter space. Sarah had begun to regret the room's extravagance even before Amy stepped into it wearing her yoga pants and Birkenstocks. But now it was clear to her that the kitchen was obscene.

"No, it's beautiful," said Amy. "Cooking here would be like visiting a spa."

"For me, it's more like boot camp," Sarah said, as she searched for a clean coffee cup.

Everyone said Amy looked fantastic. Only Sarah silently disagreed. Amy might be clothed in an earth-toned yoga costume, her hair neatly abbreviated in Soccer Mom style, but Sarah wasn't fooled. She was a trained observer, skilled at detecting the gnawed knuckles of the bulimic's manicured fingers or picking out the monster parent in the pastel family portrait. In Amy's face, she saw the hallmarks of insomnia: the twitch of caffeine in her right eyelid, the blue half-moons beneath her tired eyes.

"She's changed," she whispered to me at the coffee pot. "I can see it. Something's wrong."

"Where's Bill?" Bryn asked Amy. "And the kids?" Amy never traveled without Jeremy and Jason, Hannah and Iris.

"I came without them," Amy said, accepting the coffee Sarah offered.

"So you're running away," I joked.

"Good timing," said Linda. "Fast forward to January, when all the hoopla's over."

"I wish I could," Amy said, collapsing into a chair.

Through gentle cross-examination, Bryn established that the home Amy fled was not her own but her mother's. After we'd laughed nervously and rifled through the evidence that our own marriages were intact, Amy told us that her widowed mother had dementia. Her only sister Ellen had called her back home to help.

SEVEN

For two years, Amy had been fielding frantic calls from Ellen. Their mother, Grace, was losing things, forgetting where she'd parked her car, and shredding letters in the garbage disposal. At Thanksgiving, Grace had tried to clean up by flushing silverware down the toilet. "I don't have kids, but that doesn't mean I can be Mom's mom," Ellen had said, sounding angry and exhausted the last time she and Amy had talked.

Finally, Amy flew to Phoenix to bring her mother home with her for Christmas, possibly for longer. But after three harrowing days with her mother, she saw things as Ellen did. And yesterday, instead of driving Grace to Albuquerque as she'd promised, she'd taken her mother's keys, loaded her luggage into her old T-bird, and delivered her to the facility Ellen had chosen.

"You had to," said Bryn.

"How could I?" asked Amy, wringing her hands.

The sign for Desert Sky Living Care should have aroused Grace's suspicion; she'd feared hospitals ever since her husband died in one. But Amy parked and persuaded her mother inside with a lie about picking up a prescription for sleeping pills. "You know you can't sleep in a strange bed," she'd said, as they entered the lobby. The word "strange" had stuck in her throat. Too late, she'd realized her mother had never seen her home in Albuquerque, and wouldn't ever, now.

Grace, alerted by Amy's stammer and by the lobby's medicinal scent, caught and held her daughter's hand. "Is this it?" she asked, looking around her. "Are we here?"

Amy couldn't answer. She buried her face in Grace's ridiculous sweatshirt, which was stamped with her grandchildren's handprints in Day-Glo fabric paint. Amy would have held on to her mother forever if Ellen hadn't intervened.

"Amy, this isn't about you!" Ellen said, as she led their mother to the reception desk.

Papers were signed, permission was granted, and a wheelchair appeared from out of nowhere, followed by a bored-looking nurse. Christina Gonzalez—as her plastic nametag ID'd her—crossed the room to Amy's mother, then braked the chair and locked her hip. Grace let Ellen help her into the wheelchair, but then she twisted around abruptly, nearly launching herself onto the slick granite floor. Her eyes were wild and searching. "Please!" she said, as the nurse patted her shoulder. "Please, please, help me!"

Shamed by her deception, Amy turned and hurried away. The nearest exit was the elevator, but as she approached it, the mirrored doors closed, making a wall where there had been a way out. Who was that scowling woman? Amy asked her own reflection. She looked depleted, like a sagging hot air balloon. Amy was shocked to realize that the daughter she'd been was gone. In her place was a person who looked just like her mother, the source of the heat that had kept Amy aloft.

When she turned around again, the nurse was pushing Grace slowly toward the elevator, taking her up to her room. "Wait!" Amy cried. She dropped to her knees in front of the wheelchair and held tight to the tips of her mother's canvas shoes. "I'm sorry, Mama!" she said. "Come home with me. I can take care of you!"

But Grace only flinched and looked away. "Please keep that woman away from me," she said to the nurse. "She's been following me for years, and I don't know what she *wants*." This last word she spit like something bitter. Amy, so irrationally angry she could have strangled her mother, began instead to weep.

She expected to be shooed away any minute, but the nurse bent over her protectively and placed her hand in her mother's. "This is your daughter," the nurse said to Grace. "Your pretty daughter Amy. We played jacks together in the kitchen while you taught my mother English, do you remember? In our yellow house on Ocotillo Street?"

Amy glanced at the nurse's nametag. "Christina Gonzalez!" she said. "I apologize. I do remember! It's been a difficult day."

Nurse Gonzalez smiled at her and nodded.

"You were such a smart girl, Christina!" Grace said. "You always helped your mother with her spelling." For the first time that morning, Grace seemed at peace. "That was the best time," she said. "The best thing I ever did."

And so, for a moment, the lifeline of memory brought Amy's mother back to herself and took her to the place where she couldn't be reached.

EIGHT

No one spoke until Amy had finished her story. Some of us silently grieved. Some of us silently thanked our mothers—for the season's sake, for naming and knowing us, for blocking our paths on the road to the end. Loss always lurked beneath our conversations in Playgroup, under talk of microdermabrasion, premenopausal symptoms, IRAs and long-term health insurance. Loss was Bryn's motive to search for her birth mother, and loss was the muse for the letter to her, still unanswered, I helped Bryn to write. Loss was the mid-life alarm sounding, more and more often these days. Each of us had tried to silence its bell with something: a job change, volunteer work, a home renovation, a marathon, a novel, a new prescription, another child. We were on this road together, and the caretaking we had in common was the basis for our friendship on the journey we shared.

Maggie rose from the table and poured out second cups of coffee. Bryn broke into the box of donut holes that Sarah had bought for the kids.

"Pain," said Liza, as she pulled herself into Sarah's lap. "Pain," she insisted, pointing to the sky.

"Yes, Liza, airplane," said Sarah. All morning, she'd lied about the sound of David's circular saw, as he labored on Liza's surprise Christmas gift. She'd lied and told herself these lies were different from the lies her mother told, which masked the noise of their family's demolition.

"You said your mother's car is an old T-bird?" I asked. "Turquoise? Sarah thought she saw it parked outside."

"I drove by yesterday to look at the house," Amy said. "I wanted to come in, but I just . . . didn't."

"What about your mom's house?" asked Bryn. "Are you selling it?"

"There's still a lot of sorting to do before we can put it on the market," Amy said. Ellen had a system for disposing of her mother's relics, while Amy wanted to examine each object, pondering its history and its potential use.

"It makes me tired just thinking about it," said Linda, whose fits of household organization were always preceded by the overwhelming urge to torch her house and start again.

"You should hire a service," said Bryn, scrolling through the contacts on her phone. "I'll give you some numbers."

"Go home first," said Maggie. "It's Christmas Eve. You should be with your family." She removed the Santa Claus pin on her own lapel and clipped it to Amy's collar. Maybe because Amy didn't know Maggie, this gesture loosened the tight hold she'd had on herself since she'd returned home. Her shoulders began to shake with sobs.

"Tying," Liza said. "Bubbles on her mouf."

"Shhh," Sarah said. She leaned over and laid her hand on top of Amy's, steadying herself as she felt the wrenching turn from envy to sympathy. We all dreaded the day our children would grow up and leave us, but it was unthinkable that a mother could forget her own child. Unthinkable, that is, for everyone but Sarah. Later, she told me that when she'd taken Amy's hand, she'd known that whatever happened with her baby, she would be able to face it. She'd prepared all her life to rely on herself.

* * *

Life is change.

That was the true subject of Sarah's next painting, though for a long time, she thought it was about choosing between her child and her work. Her anxiety wasn't surprising. Sarah was just eight years old when she lost her mother, too young for a lesson that most of us need a lifetime to learn. Isn't that what art is for? To let us look and think and look again, until we finally see?

That morning, the air outside seemed filled with phantoms. An indifferent wind moved a few dry, curled leaves along the sidewalk. Empty houses receded in parallel lines toward the vanishing point. The scene was exactly as Sarah had dreamt it, and exactly as she would paint it eventually. In the sky, birds, compelled by unknown forces, flew away in formation, each one alone but surrounded by comrades who gave shape to their flight. Old grief and new yearning seized Sarah as she stood at the curb with the rest of us, watching Amy Marley set off for Albuquerque in her mother's ghost car, traveling into the future where her own children waited.

NINE

Face to face in Sarah's baby book are two pictures taken three months later, in the spring. The first photo is of Charlie, Sarah's son, on the happy day when he was born perfectly healthy. The second photo is of Liza, eating cake at her second birthday party. Suddenly, Sarah was an ordinary mother again. Like all of us, she'd worry vaguely about her children's well-being for the rest of her life. But always present in her mind was what she'd understood when Amy Marley returned on Christmas Eve. Then, when the mass was still unresolved, Sarah felt exceptional. She was alone, isolated even from her husband, as I imagine parents who've lost a child feel.

She couldn't go back. She went forward, knowing what she knew.

TEN

Sarah's father, Sam Holloway, had gotten remarried to a woman named Cheryl, who ironed his shirts and cleaned his house and shopped for the dinner request he phoned in every afternoon. Cheryl reminded Sarah of Krazy, who still piled socks by the back door whenever she and David went out. What she'd thought at first was a tribute now seemed, three months later, like a sad little prayer meant to bring them home.

Whenever Cheryl drank too much, as she did at Liza's birthday party at David's parents' house, she'd tell how her own father had collapsed at his desk at 47, leaving her mother incapacitated by grief. She'd had to raise her five younger siblings, which gave her a handbook full of advice she never hesitated to share. "Those veggies could choke her," she'd said when Liza grabbed for the crudités I'd brought along with my daughter Hannah, the only guest Liza's age. "That coffee table needs some bumpers," she'd chided our hosts, until David's father padded its cut-glass corners with gauze pads and surgical tape. "Watch the dog!" she'd warned Sarah, meaning Gusto, the Furys' black lab, who lay still as a bear rug next to baby Charlie's carrier.

It was an odd setting for a toddler's birthday party: home to a large dog and numerous choking hazards and breakable objects, a place that Sarah called *La Maison Dangereuse*. Better, though, than Sarah's home. The electrician had just pulled the ceiling from their kitchen to replace the tangle of old wiring she'd feared might spark and flame one day, bringing the whole house down.

"No, honey, that's Grandma's juice," Cheryl warned, as Liza made a grab for her margarita, Cheryl's third. Sarah drank orange juice because she was nursing, and I drank it with her out of sympathy.

"Lighten up, Cheryl," said Frank Fury, hoisting the pitcher for another pass. He winked at Liza, who monkeyed him, holding her own eye shut. "It's your birthday, kid," he said. "You might as well live it up."

"When David was little, I let him sip from my daiquiri," said David's mother, Jocelyn. "Look at him! He survived."

"Just barely," David said, covering his glass with his palm.

Frank passed over Cheryl's glass without stopping, though she'd scooted it forward an inch. "Well, you're lucky," Cheryl said. "Listen, I know what I'm talking about. I may not have my own kids, but I raised that whole brood in Yuma."

"You sure did," said Sarah's father. He sat cross-legged on the floor, assembling Liza's new trike. The toy was way beyond the child's abilities, like most of the gifts from the Furys so far.

The Furys always overdid it with Liza, while the Holloways gave her only what Sarah put on a list: fire-retardant pajamas, a sweater for spring, and a set of safety gates. Each gift came with Sam's long, boring story of conquest, as though he were Meriwether Lewis in the wilderness of the suburban mall. His many years of teaching astronomy at Arizona State had assured him that his audience would sit through the dullest recounting of facts. I thought his students must have hoped he'd veer off the topic for once and explore the mysteries of the universe. But he was 63, nearing retirement, and Sarah said it hadn't happened yet.

Jocelyn pulled a fifty from her wallet, saying, "I wanted to get Liza a baby doll, but this week at the office was nuts."

"Mom, you've already given her too much," David said, just as Liza snatched the bill from her hand.

"Money!" she said.

"I don't know where she learned that

word," Sarah said. In fact, she often used the term to describe David's parents to the Playgroup—and to explain what they made at their advertising agency, Mirage.

"Big money!" Hannah said, spreading her arms wide. Liza shrieked at their private joke.

Like Phoenix, the Furys thrived on the rumor of riches. While David joined historic commissions to save the old horse trails and adobe dwellings, his parents remade the city's image with photos of sparkling swimming pools and words like "majestic" and "haute."

"Liza, give the money to Mommy," Jocelyn said. "She'll buy you a pretty Barbie. Mr. Luddite will just blow it on some sad little rag doll."

"Mr. Luddite? This guy?" I said, pointing to David. "The man who couldn't live without the Diaper Houdini?"

"It's one of the century's greatest inventions," David said. "Right up there with the Internet."

"I wonder what people did before they had the technology to turn their used Pampers into airtight sausages," Sarah said.

"We soaked them in Borax, that's what," Cheryl said. Her face had a rapturous expression, as though the stench of ammonia defined the good old days. "We washed them in scalding hot water and hung them out to dry in the sun."

"Not me! I had a service," Jocelyn said.

"Those were cloth diapers, of course,"

Cheryl said. "And once your kids were toilet trained, you could use them for dust rags."

I tried to remember the last time I'd dusted. Definitely before Hannah was born. Back then, the urge to clean had overwhelmed me. I'd organized closets, mopped the floor at midnight, even put ancient vacation photos in albums. Our underwear still had holes from my enthusiastic use of bleach. Then one night I put Cole to sleep on bleached-white, clean-smelling sheets. By morning, his cheeks were scarlet. It was all the proof I needed that I was actually harming my son with housekeeping meant to make his world safe. Hannah had her brother to thank for the saner mother she had. You laugh more with your second child.

That's what I'd told Sarah—after all the tests showed that the mass in Charlie's belly was gone. But even now, with the cancer scare behind her, Sarah worried. She worried about undertows, world war, bright-colored plastics piling up in landfills, crafty kangaroo rats bringing back the bubonic plague. She knew her fears were unreasonable, but she held on to them just in case. David contained his fears efficiently by investing in gadgets like the Diaper Houdini.

"Time for cake," said Jocelyn, swaying a bit as she rose from her seat. To keep Cheryl from offering, she added quickly, "Frank, come get the plates."

Liza took off after her grandparents, but Cheryl blocked her path. "Not so fast, Missy," she said. "The kitchen is a boo-boo place."

"Daddy!" Liza cried, as she ran to David. Cheryl scared her—Hannah, too. Those little girls knew the power of *No*. In Cheryl, they'd met their match.

David caught Liza and gently flipped her over, so that the ends of her hair touched the floor. Liza was perfectly still for a moment, stunned by her father's strength. "Daddy has insect vision that lets him see you from any angle," he told her, "and bat radar that lets him anticipate your every move."

"No!" said Liza, when he set her down again. "Out!" Her eyes were on the pool in the backyard.

"It's locked," David said to Sarah. "I checked."

"Oh boy, could I tell you stories about drownings," Cheryl said.

"Please don't," Sarah said. "We heard enough at our CPR and Child Safety class."

Everyone in Playgroup had taken the same course. "God! That was like reading the *Encyclopedia Morticia*," I said.

"It's good to know, though, isn't it?" said Cheryl, picking at the taped table's edge.

"I wish I didn't," said Sarah, though I knew she was bluffing. She took heed from many sources, including the messes her clients' ambitious parents made of their children's lives. "The nurse seemed to enjoy scaring us," Sarah said. "She acted like she was the only thing standing between us and our kid dying from drinking Mr. Clean."

"I'm sure she didn't enjoy it," said Cheryl, taking a sip of Sam's drink.

"She preyed on our superstition," Sarah said. "Child-proofing my house doesn't mean my child will be safe."

"You mean you don't lock up your cleaners?" said Cheryl.

"Of course I do!"

"So taking the safety course was a good idea."

"At least that way, you're ready," said Sam. He still armed himself with information, though nothing had prepared him for his wife to leave her family, and knowing how his son died didn't bring him any peace.

As they argued, David helped Liza onto the tricycle. The pedals were still three inches beyond her reach, though, and she was quickly frustrated as she tried to move forward by kicking the air. David lifted her gently back to the floor and showed her how to steer the trike as she walked beside it. Her dignity restored, Liza was calmed.

But Cheryl couldn't let it go. "Bad things happen to test your faith," she said.

"Bad things happen randomly," Sarah said. "And those poor people who say they're telling their sad story to help you are just trying to find a reason why it happened to them."

"Some people think superstition is the foundation for faith," said Sam.

"Some people, Dad?" asked Sarah. "That's what *you* think." She teased, though she hummed "Amazing Grace" as she buckled Charlie into his car seat or cut Liza's meals into pieces smaller than her windpipe. She'd told me she was considering going to church again.

"Your father goes to church every Sunday," said Cheryl.

"Our cat brings us socks every time we leave the house," David said. "She puts them by the door, like an offering. Sarah says she's praying. But maybe Krazy knows we'll come home, and she's just keeping busy until we do."

"Keeping busy is a kind of prayer," Sarah said.

I knew what she meant. There's a certainty of purpose to childcare that's comforting: Feed, dress, change, play, feed, nap, change, walk, feed, change, bath, book, bed, sleep; repeat. All the parenting books say that children thrive on routine, but no one talks about the way routine keeps you moored to your life as a mother.

"But Krazy doesn't have to worry that she's wasting her time," David said, "since she knows for sure we exist."

ELEVEN

The Furys began a chorus of "Happy Birthday" as they came back into the living room carrying an exquisite bakery cake. The instant they'd finished singing, Cheryl blew out the candle so Liza wouldn't get burned.

The cake was spread with white fondant, its smooth surface ruptured by the candle, an enormous, leaning numeral two. "It looks like Puerto del Sol," David joked, meaning the new "luxury homes" crammed into what had been the old Murphy estate. He'd appealed to every potential sponsor in Phoenix to save it, but ended up with nothing but a small pile of authentic adobe bricks and a rusted horse bridle he'd found in the grass where the barn had been.

"In five years, you'll forget the Murphy place ever existed," Frank said. His good friend Wyn Beacham had financed the project, a sore point with his son. "And in fifty years, your little Liza will be rabble-rousing to save Puerto del Sol."

"That's depressing," Sarah said. She wasn't thinking of the graceless subdivision, but of her infant son a half-century old, her baby daughter fifty-two. She would be eighty, then.

"I don't know, Dad," David said. "What's the life expectancy of particle board?" He was smiling, though the loss of the historical property had been devastating to him.

Jocelyn rolled her eyes. "Every generation thinks they're going to save the earth," she said. She plucked the candle from the icing and began to cut the cake.

"First cut out a circle in the middle," Cheryl said. "That way, all the pieces will be the same size."

"To hell with that," Frank said. "I want a big piece!"

"Too much sugar isn't good for the girls," Cheryl said. Jocelyn nodded, and served up two identically huge hunks for Liza and Hannah.

"Pick one," Sarah said, showing them the slices side by side. When each girl was sure she had the larger share, they took a few bites and left the plates on the table to circle the room with the trike.

"Smooth," I said.

"Thanks," said Sarah. "That's what Amy Marley would do."

Gusto, roused by the clink-scrape of silver against china, raised his noble head. "Uh-oh," said Cheryl. "Where's the baby?"

"He's right here," David said. "Safe and sound. And asleep."

"Shirley, quit making everyone crazy," Jocelyn said. "Gusto's a very gentle dog."

"Cheryl," said Cheryl. "Every dog is gentle. Until the dog bites."

Hearing his name, Gusto hauled himself to a standing position, shaking out old, arthritic limbs. He assembled himself the way you would a folding card table, his broad back rising, legs locking stiffly into place beneath. “Gusto comes from a long line of castle dogs,” Frank said, as he tempted the dog with dessert served on a gold-edged Wedgwood plate. “His ancestors kept the vermin away by sitting under the table and eating the scraps.”

“He’s the right dog for the job,” I said. We watched as Gusto took the cake in one bite and then licked the plate clean, pushing it across the carpet with his muscled tongue.

“Oh! There’s one more present!” Cheryl said. With her foot, she nudged a package out from under the table. It was obviously from the Holloways, wrapped in paper printed with kittens chasing balls of string. The gift’s sudden, sly movement caught Gusto's attention, and he began to growl.

"Watch the baby!" warned Cheryl, and Charlie, who'd slept through the entire party so far, raised his arms like a goalie and started to wail.

"He might be hungry," Sarah said, as she stood and scooped Charlie up in his carrier. "Gusto, would you like to go out?" The dog was at the sliding glass door in two seconds flat, panting and dancing in circles.

David's parents kept the pool heated for Gusto until April, so the water was often warmer than the air. When Sarah opened the door, the dog bounded to the pool and descended to the second step. He stood there looking out from the mist that rose from the water's surface, as solemn as a water buffalo.

"It's cold outside," Cheryl said. "Are you sure it's okay for him to get wet?" When no one answered, she sing-songed sarcastically, "I guess so."

"I'm going to feed Charlie," Sarah said to David, as she slid the door closed. "Keep an eye on Liza."

"Let's get on with it," Frank said. He looked at his watch, anticipating a televised Diamondbacks game.

"There's a story behind that gift," Sam said.

"Refill," I said, grabbing my glass. I slipped into the kitchen behind Sarah, just as her father began again to retrace his steps, hoping to prove how hard he'd tried.

* * *

In the kitchen, the orange juice carton lay empty on its side on the counter. Just as I'd suspected, it had been an afterthought for the teetotalers, hastily retrieved from the back of the fridge. Sarah set Charlie's carrier on the counter and filled her glass with water from the tap. "Save me!" she said to Charlie, stroking his fat cheek.

"You weren't kidding," I said. "What a bunch of characters."

"Put them in your book," she said. "Thank God you're here."

Behind her, the ice cream freezer hummed and churned, mixing Frank's margaritas and lulling her son back to sleep. This batch had been forgotten. The gears labored in the thickening mixture;

the drink brimmed the top of the metal canister like a jagged iceberg. I switched off the machine and filled up my glass. "Cheers," I said. Sarah got a spoon from the drawer.

"Tastes like I'm twenty," she said.

"Dancing at Carumba's," I said. "Kissing strangers."

"Riding the bus home from my crappy job at that tacky art gallery."

"The one with the velvet paintings?"

"Worse," she said. "DeGrazia. Old Mexico meets Rainbow Brite."

"There's one hanging in their bathroom," I said. "Madonna and Child."

Sarah nodded. "They're originally from Ohio," she said, as if that explained everything.

Sarah's vision was darker, nothing you'd want to hang on the wall. One picture in particular haunted her: her childhood home at Christmas, like a burnt-out bulb in a circuit of neighboring rooflines traced in colored lights. The house where her brother had shot himself. Who could blame Sarah for painting over it? Even I sometimes revised the fairy tales I read to Cole and Hannah—giving ogres hidden virtues and princesses fatal flaws—to make the world safe with my words. But this was a false and temporary power. My children would grow up, but I'd never get back my old courage, which I'd put away inside a long box with my wedding dress and my singular self.

"Remember when we were fearless?" I said.

"Not me. I was terrified," Sarah said. She rinsed the spoon under hot water, dried it, and replaced it in the drawer. When she glanced up, out the kitchen window, she saw Liza running across the pool deck flapping her arms, trying to fly.

"Liza! she screamed.

Hannah, I thought. I grabbed Charlie and followed Sarah out of the kitchen. To my relief, I found my daughter on the safe side of the open glass door, holding Cheryl's hand.

"It's a good thing I was here," Cheryl said.

"Hannah's afraid of water," I said, bracing my trembling leg with the weight of Charlie's carrier. "She wouldn't ever go near the pool."

"Doggie swim!" said Hannah, pointing to Gusto excitedly. Gusto had leapt from the water and knocked Liza to the deck before she could fall into the pool. Now he circled her, wagging his tail, waiting for someone to tell him if he was a good dog or bad.

David got there before Sarah did. He picked Liza up and paced back and forth as her tears soaked his shoulder, as if he were looking for someone to blame.

"I thought I locked it," I heard Sarah say.

"I wasn't watching," David said.

"She's all right, it's all right," Sarah said, stroking Liza's arm.

"The pool is a big owie, Liza! So big

that Daddy would feel it," David said. His voice was angry and loud.

"Mama!" Liza cried.

Sarah took her daughter and rocked her, kissing the top of her head. Eventually, Liza stopped crying and David brought her back inside. But Sarah lingered in the yard a while longer, as if by studying the scene, something could be learned.

TWELVE

Sarah was careful to lock the door behind her when she came back in to the living room. David and his parents were on the couch watching the baseball game, with Charlie curled on David's chest. I sat on the floor with Hannah, who patted Gusto's head and babbled to him, recounting his heroic deed. Cheryl made herself conspicuously useful, cleaning up bits of curled ribbon and discarded wrapping paper.

Sarah's father held Liza in the armchair and sang to her softly, "Home on the Range." She'd said that the sentimental cowboy song was the first she'd ever learned, sitting outside on a picnic table with her father, singing and looking up at the stars. That had been before her mother left them, but even then, Sarah had been more aware of the danger outside her father's sheltering arms than the safety within. Liza was relaxed with her grandfather, though. Sarah paused and closed her eyes before she joined them, as if she were praying to preserve her daughter's ease. "Home, home, home," Liza sang, looking up at Sam as her mother must have once, transfixed by his voice, not yet understanding his words.